Oranges and Giraffes
A Story About Friends

By PAM ROBBINS

Illustrated by
TONY HUFNAGEL

Lulu.com

Robbins, Pam

Oranges and Giraffes

A Story About Friends

ISBN 978-1-300-97970-8

Published by Lulu.com

Printed and bound in the United States of America

Acknowledgements

Thanks to Sally Boutiette, who gave me a good idea with just one phrase; Annie Emanuelli, who helped me turn a good idea into a book (again); and Kristy Dunning—who had room in her heart for another friend.

*M*olly Lee started crying the minute she got off the
school bus on Monday. Nobody saw her tears
except her mother. She was glad about that.

"What happened?" said her mother, Margaret.
"What's wrong?"

"*J*enny was mean to me today," Molly said.
It hurt to even say it. Molly and Jenny had been
friends since they were 3 and now they were in the
same grade in school. Molly thought they would
be friends till they grew up—maybe forever.

"*W*hat did Jenny do?" her mother asked Molly.

"She told me to sit someplace else at lunch and she didn't ask me to play tag," Molly said. "She has a new friend she likes better than me." Molly began to cry even harder.

 Margaret Lee put her hand on Molly's shoulder as they walked from the bus stop to their house. Together they went past their driveway, up three steps and through the red door. They were home.

Her mother gave Molly a glass of juice and seated her at the kitchen table. Molly helped her mother roll out cookie dough and then she read until supper. She felt better by the time she went to bed.

But the next morning she had a belly ache. It wasn't a sick belly ache. It was a scared belly ache. She wished it was Saturday so that she wouldn't have to go to school.

She didn't even want to get on the bus that morning. She had always sat beside Jenny and today she wouldn't know where to sit.

"This will be the hardest day," her mother told her. "Maybe you and Jenny will make up and maybe you won't, but by tomorrow, it will be a little easier. I promise."

As she waited at the corner for the bus, Molly thought and thought about what her mother told her. She hoped that it was true.

Two boys were waiting for the bus, too. They both said hi to her but it didn't help. When the bus came, she got on and took the very first empty seat.

She saw her mother speak to the bus monitor. The monitor nodded and then smiled at Molly but Molly could not smile back.

She didn't look at Jenny or anyone else. She didn't even wave goodbye to her mother. She looked straight ahead until the bus driver stopped in front of the school and opened the door.

Molly got off the bus right behind the monitor and walked into the building by herself. She was the first one to take her seat in her classroom.

"*G*ood morning," her teacher said. "Good morning," Molly said.

*S*he liked her teacher and was usually happy to talk to her, but she didn't say much after that. She felt very sad all day.

Last night, her mom had said, "Maybe you and Jenny will be friends again. Maybe you will find a new friend. I don't know, Molly, and you don't know. I do know you will be all right. Try to keep a hopeful heart."

Molly did try to keep a hopeful heart. The teacher told her she did good work on her spelling test.

That was nice, but Jenny didn't talk to her all day.

So by the time she got home from school, Molly was almost crying again. The same thing happened on Wednesday.

Then on Thursday, a girl named Sara with straight black hair and brown eyes asked Molly if she wanted to see her new doll.

She was not sure what to say because she didn't really know Sara very well, but she said yes.

She and Sara talked and played together for a little while and they had a lot of fun.

Molly wasn't as sad when she got off the bus that afternoon. She said to her mother. "I played with a girl named Sara today. She's very nice." Her mother smiled.

Molly and Sara played at recess Friday and all the next week. They ate lunch together, too. Jenny had a new friend—and so did Molly.

The next week, Sara's mother called Molly's mother and invited Molly for a sleepover. When Molly heard the news, she was very quiet. She didn't look as happy as she should, and her mother asked her why.

Molly said in a small voice, "I'm scared, Mommy. I thought Jenny was my friend. And now she isn't. What if Sara does the same thing Jenny did?"

*H*er mother pulled her onto her lap even though she was way too big for that. There was no one to see, so it was all right.

"*C*omparing Jenny to Sara is like comparing oranges to giraffes," Margaret Lee said. Molly giggled.

"*M*ommy, that's silly," she said. "An orange is a fruit and a giraffe is an animal. They aren't the same at all. Everybody knows that.

"*B*esides, Jenny is not round or orange. And Sara does not have a long neck or spots." She and her mother laughed and laughed at that.

*T*hen her mother said, "I know, but that is just how silly it is to compare Sara to Jenny. They are not the same at all, either. I remember that Jenny likes to ride her bike and play with her dog and watch TV.

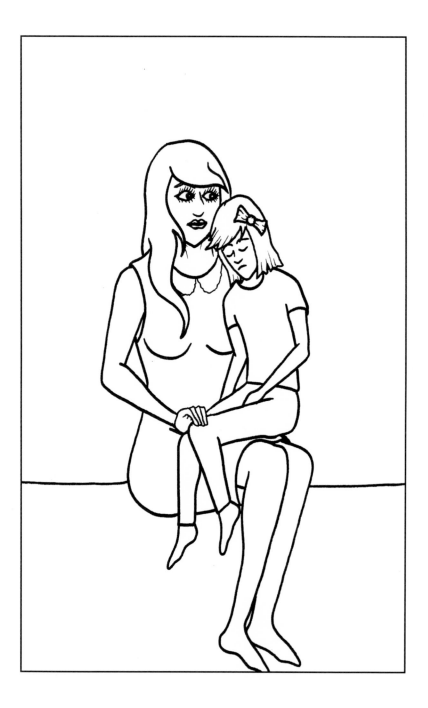

"You told me that Sara likes to draw and play with her cat and read." Molly nodded. That was true.

"They are very different girls in those ways—and in lots of other ways, too," her mother said. "Do you see?" Molly thought about that.

"I get it," she told her mother. "Our last cat, Lucky, was orange with double paws. He liked to be held. But Kitty hates to be held and she is white and black. Even cats are not all the same, right?"

"That's exactly right, Molly. So there's no reason to think Sara will hurt your feelings just because Jenny did."

Molly slid off her mother's lap, but her mother took her hand. "You know, even if you and Jenny are not friends right now, you were good friends for a while and that's a good thing. You might even be friends again some day. Nobody knows."

"Some friends are friends for a short time, and some for a long time," Mrs. Lee said. "Some, like your Auntie Pat and I, are friends for life."

"Do you know what it means to be unique, Molly? It means to be one of a kind. Each person is unique. So you have to give each person a chance. Don't be afraid to do that. For now, just try to remember the fun you had with Jenny and wish her a happy life. And you have a happy life, too."

Then she asked, "Do you really like Sara?"

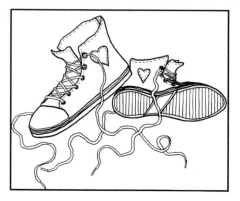

"Yes, I do, Mommy," Molly said. "I like her a lot. Sara shares all her stuff, and we have so much fun. We both like school, and animals—especially pandas and penguins—and we have the same pink sneakers."

"Well," Margaret Lee said. "It sounds like you have a wonderful new friend who is just right for you." Molly nodded.

She understood what her mother was saying, but inside she was still a little bit afraid.

Maybe it would be better if she just played by herself, or with her dolls and Kitty, she thought. That way, she would never have to lose another friend. She didn't ever want to feel so sad again.

She didn't say that to her mother, but her mother knew what she was thinking. Mothers know a lot of things.

That night, Margaret Lee tucked Molly into bed and then sat down beside her.

"I want to tell you a story," she said, and so she began.

Once upon a time, there were two giraffes that lived in a zoo not far from here.

Most giraffes like to live in Africa but these two were born in the United States. They had always lived in the zoo and they were very happy there.

One day, one of the giraffes noticed that a little mouse lived under a bush right outside the giraffe enclosure. That is a big word for the pen where animals live in the zoo.

Because the giraffe, whose name was Jerry, had such a long neck, he could see the little creature almost without trying.

It made his heart sad to see how alone and afraid the mouse always looked. There were others like it, but it kept to itself.

It feared thunder and lightning, tigers and lions, cats and dogs—even dogs walking quietly with people, and most noises.

The mouse was afraid of all sorts of things.

Jerry thought that maybe being afraid so much came from being alone so much.

Jerry told Gina, the giraffe he lived with, all about the little mouse.

Gina said she thought it was very sad but then she didn't seem to give it another thought.

So Jerry made a plan.

One day he called to the mouse, being sure to keep his voice soft.

"Hey, are you OK, little one? Do you need a friend?"

The tiny mouse, a girl, was amazed that the giraffe could even see her sitting there so many feet below him.

"I guess so," she said, shyly.

The giraffe nodded. His long neck moved every time his head did. "I know so," he said.

"You are alone too much in your little nest."

"If you could get up to this branch next to my head, we could see each other better and talk and maybe we could be friends."

From where she was, on the ground, the branch seemed very high, but the mouse liked the sound of being friends.

So she took a deep breath, dug her tiny claws into the tree and began to climb.

In a few minutes, the mouse was sitting on a branch near the giraffe's head.

Looking back at her were the biggest eyes— with the longest eyelashes—she had ever seen.

The giraffe was happy to be able to see the mouse up close.

"Hi," he said. "You made it. That was brave."

The mouse felt shy. "You made me brave. I was afraid, but I wanted to get to know you. So I decided to try."

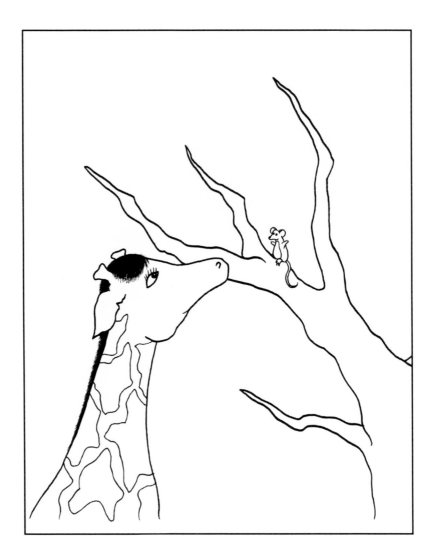

"You did great," the giraffe said. "You'll be glad you did. We're going to have a lot of fun."

"What's your name? Are you a girl or a boy? We are kind of different and will have to find things we both can do, but we will. Don't worry."

The mouse felt warm inside. She was so happy. "I am a girl but nobody ever gave me a name," she told the giraffe.

Jerry thought for a moment. "There is a little girl who comes here all the time. Her name is Mia. It means my.

"Is that a good name? Do you like it?"

The mouse was almost jumping for joy. She had a name and she had a friend.

Then she got quiet. "There is something...."
She paused, and then went on. "You should
know that I tried to have a friend before. It
didn't go very well.

"Bigger creatures chased me. Smaller
creatures feared me. Me! Smarter creatures
made me feel not so smart. I didn't find anyone
who wanted to be my friend for very long."

The giraffe blinked away a tear. He could see
how sad she was. "Well, I want to be your
friend for a long time," he said. "And if
anything tries to harm you, I will stand up for
you the best I can."

"But why would you do that?" the mouse said.
"You have a friend who looks just like you and
lives right beside you. Why would you need a
friend like me? What can I do for you?" she
asked.

"*I can't protect you. I am too small,*" *she said.* "*I can't even walk with you. It would take me hours to catch up.*

"*I think you would be a great friend but I would not,*" *she said sadly. The little mouse felt awful, sure that the giraffe would change his mind about wanting to be her friend.*

"*What can you do for me?*" *Jerry said. He thought about it for a minute.*

"*Well, you can visit me whenever you like. You can keep me company. That's important for friends to do.*

"*Gina, the other giraffe, is my friend. You are right about that. But I have room in my heart for another friend.*"

Jerry the giraffe had more to say.

"You can drop off that branch and sit on top of my head and that way we can walk together. You can tell me your stories and listen to my stories.

"We will watch the breeze in the trees and listen to the rain and enjoy the warm sun and the cool shade," he told Mia.

"We will pass the time together. That is what friends do.

"You can count on me," Jerry said. "That will make me feel very useful and very happy."

Jerry gave Mia a moment to take in all the things he had said to her. Then he asked her a very important question.

"So what do you think? Do you want to be friends?"

"*W*hat do you think, Molly?" she heard her mother
ask again. For a minute, she thought the giraffe
was talking to her.

"*D*id Mia say yes or no to having a new friend?"
her mother asked softly.

Molly opened her sleepy eyes a little and smiled. "I think she said yes," she said. Then she went to sleep.

The next morning at breakfast, Molly had trouble sitting still. She wanted to hurry and get to school.

"You know what?" she said, taking a bite of toast. Her mother waited for her to go on.

"Oranges are nice but there are a lot of them. Almost everybody who wants an orange can have one," Molly said.

"Not everybody can even *know* a giraffe," she said.

"Sara is like a giraffe because she is special. Right, Mommy?" Her mother smiled. "Right, Molly." Molly hugged her mother. "When I get home from school today, I am going to make a picture of a giraffe for Sara. It will be a surprise.

"When I give it to her, I'll tell her about oranges and giraffes. Do you think that's a good idea, Mommy?"

Molly didn't wait for an answer. She was too excited.

"I have to go. I want to tell Sara that I feel lucky to have her for a friend," she said as she ran out the door. Her mother could hardly catch up with her.

Molly did draw the picture for Sara. She began by drawing a very nice giraffe. She put a bright sun and some birds in the sky, and then she colored it all carefully.

*H*er mother found a pretty pink frame for her and helped her wrap the picture in gift paper. When they were finished, Molly was very happy. It's always fun to make a present for a friend.

Sara really liked the picture—and the story about what it meant. She and Molly put lots of glitter on the frame.

Then Sara's mother hung the picture over Sara's desk in her room. It was there for a very long time.

Only Molly and Sara and their moms ever knew the true meaning of the picture. That's why it made them all smile whenever they looked at it.

Molly and Sara are still friends today. They understand that we can have room in our hearts for a lot of friends, and that every friend is unique – one of a kind.

*M*olly also knows that if a friend does not want to be your friend any longer, it's OK.

*Y*ou can remember the good times you shared, wish her a happy life and make a new friend—or two.

*Y*ou also should remember that your best friends are always going to be more like giraffes than oranges—because they are so very special.

The End

In memory of Lucia,
and for all the giraffes in my life,
wherever they may be.
                                    P.R.

About the Author

Pam Robbins has a master's degree in language and literature and worked as a journalist for more than 30 years.

She is the author of "Laughing Matters: Selected Columns by Humorist Pam Robbins" and "Abiding Sorrow: A Daughter's Account of Loss and Grief," and contributed to "Chicken Soup for the Mother & Daughter Soul."

She lives in western Massachusetts. This is her first book for children.

About the Illustrator

Tony Hufnagel lives in Chicopee, Mass., and is a graduate of Chicopee Comprehensive High School.

He is a largely self-taught artist who works primarily in pen and ink.

This book is his first project as an illustrator, and represents a departure from his usual style and subject matter.